SERIOUSLY SILLY

SCARY
FAIRY TALES

HANSEL and GRETEL
and the SPACE WITCH

ORCHARD BOOKS
338 Euston Road, London NW1 3BH
Orchard Books Australia
Level 17/207 Kent Street, Sydney, NSW 2000

First published in 2014 by Orchard Books
This paperback edition published in 2015

ISBN 978 1 40832 960 3

Text © Laurence Anholt 2014
Illustrations © Arthur Robins 2014

A CIP catalogue record for this book is available
from the British Library.

1 3 5 7 9 10 8 6 4 2

Printed and bound by CPI Group (UK) Ltd, Croydon, CR0 4YY

Orchard Books is a division of Hachette Children's Books,
an Hachette UK company.

www.hachette.co.uk

SCARY
FAIRY TALES

HANSEL and GRETEL and the SPACE WITCH

Laurence Anholt
& Arthur Robins

ORCHARD

www.anholt.co.uk

GOOD EVENING, FANS OF FEAR. My name is THE MAN WITHOUT A HEAD. Of course I have a head really... It's just that my head is DETACHABLE! I like to bounce it up and down like a football.

So, you like SCARY STORIES, do you? Well I warn you, the stories I am about to tell are so TERRIFYING that grown men have been known to do wee wees in their panties.

Are there any witches at your school? Perhaps they are good at spelling! Yes, go ahead and laugh, but the witch in tonight's story is not so amusing.

Do you ever look up at the starry sky and wonder if there are other creatures out there? Would they be friendly aliens who would like to share our world? Or would they be evil creatures from another world, who feed on the bones of small children?… Creatures like the SPACE WITCH!

There were once two children named Hansel and Gretel. You could not hope to meet sweeter, kinder or happier little infants. Whenever their father thought of them, tears of joy would fill his twinkly old eyes.

It is hard to believe that anyone would want to take those dear little children, cram them into a home-made space craft and launch them into the cold darkness of outer space. But that is exactly what happened, Ladies and Gentlemen.

The following tale is ABSOLUTELY TRUE and it is also UTTERLY HORRIFYING. Fasten your seat belts and prepare to set off for…the most PETRIFYING RIDE OF YOUR LIFE!

Hansel and Gretel's father was a gentle man named Larry Lambsbottom. In the front room of their tiny house, he owned a wool shop. But sadly, business was not good. People did not want to buy wool or knitting needles anymore; so Larry Lambsbottom sat in the empty shop, knitting sweaters for his two dear children.

"I have not sold a single ball of wool today," he sighed, "but at least Hansel and Gretel will be warm." The more time Larry had to spare, the more he knitted, and the bigger the children's sweaters became.

What a delightful family, you might think – they are poor, but they are happy. Well, think again, dear reader! At the back of the tiny house was a garden, and in the garden was a strange old shed. And in the strange old shed sat Hansel and Gretel's strange old stepmother, Ms Luna Tick.

Luna was a cruel and hard-hearted woman, but she was also clever. Can you guess what she did in her strange old shed? That's right! Luna Tick built space rockets, which she launched into the night sky.

"Ah haaar haar harr!"

At first, the passengers in Luna's rockets were dolls and action men, which she stole from Hansel and Gretel's bedroom. But then she began to send little animals into space – a baby snail she found in the garden and at last, Bunion, Gretel's pet rabbit.

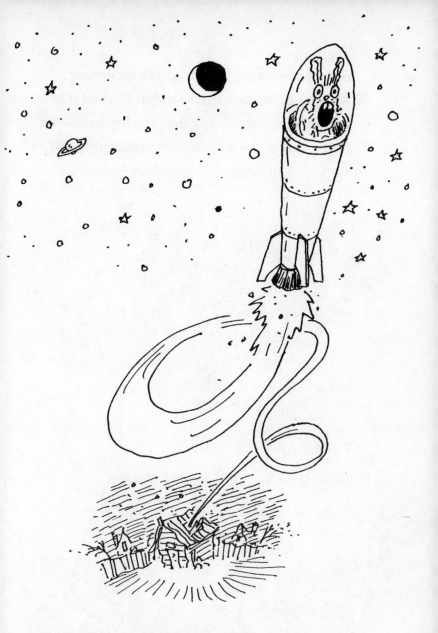

You see what a beastly woman she was!

One afternoon, Luna finished building the biggest, most powerful space rocket she had ever created. She was absolutely delighted and she began to look around for some passengers…

At this very moment, Larry Lambsbottom was locking up the wool shop. Once again, there had been no customers, so he had spent the whole day knitting a colossal yellow and purple sweater for Hansel.

"Hansel! Hansel! Come and see what I have made."

Luna watched silently as the boy skipped to his father and pulled on the huge sweater. An evil thought crept into her mind.

That evening when the children had gone to bed, she called her husband.

"Come here, Larry, you little knit. That shop of yours is useless. I've had enough of your woolly ideas. I have a plan, which will bring us loads of money – Hansel and Gretel will be the first children in outer space! Ah haaar haar harr!"

"My poor children," sighed Larry, "but at least they'll have nice sweaters to keep them warm in the infinite cosmos."

Luna led the children down the garden. There stood the huge space rocket, poking through the open roof of her shed.

Rubbing their sleepy eyes, Hansel and Gretel squeezed into the cockpit and fastened their seat belts. They looked out of the window and saw their father's sad face and their stepmother preparing for take-off.

"Five, four, three, two, one…BLAST OFF!" she screeched. "Ah haaar haar harr!"

Then the rocket began to shake and tremble until it left the ground and blasted into the night sky.

"Oh, Hansel," sobbed Gretel. "How will we ever get home?"

"Don't worry, Gretel," replied Hansel. "Look at the sweater Father made me… It is getting smaller and smaller. That's because I caught one end of it on a nail on Luna's shed, and now my sweater is unwinding behind us."

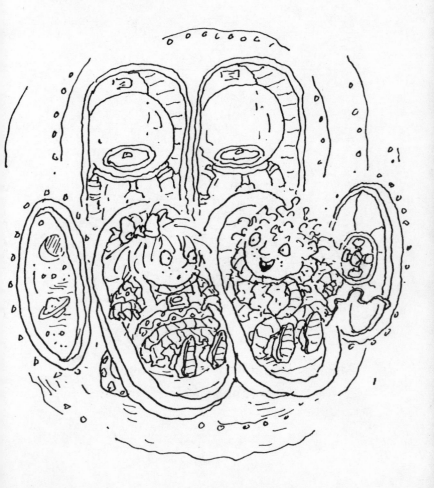

It was true! The huge sweater was unravelling behind the rocket. As they left the earth's atmosphere, Gretel could see that her clever brother had only one arm of his sweater left. Quickly she leapt forward and caught the end of the thread and held on tight.

Suddenly, the space rocket stopped. It began to turn on its orbit. The children looked out of the porthole, and to their joy, they realised they were returning to earth.

Below them, Hansel and Gretel could see the oceans and countries of the world. Then as they grew closer, they could see the twinkling lights of their own house, with Luna's shed in the garden. Suddenly there was a loud bang and the rocket crashed through the roof of the shed.

The tip of the rocket was badly dented, but the children were not hurt. They climbed down the ladder and ran into their father's arms. Luna was furious. Her rocket was damaged and her evil plan had failed.

The weeks went by. The family was poorer than ever, but Larry was content to have his children home. He spent his time knitting a new sweater for Gretel and this one was bigger and woollier than ever.

One evening, when the children were in bed, Luna said, "Guess what, Larry? I have built a new rocket. Don't look so sheepish, this time nothing can go wrong. People will flock to hear about Hansel and Gretel, the first children in outer space!"

Once again, Luna led the sleepy children down the garden path to the shed. The new space rocket was taller and more powerful than ever. Luna pushed the poor children up the ladder and into their seats.

"Five, four, three, two, one…BLAST OFF!" she screeched. "Ah haaar haar harr!"

Again, the rocket shook and trembled and roared until it left the ground and blasted into the night sky.

"Oh, Gretel," sobbed Hansel, as the rocket raced through the sky. "However will we get home?"

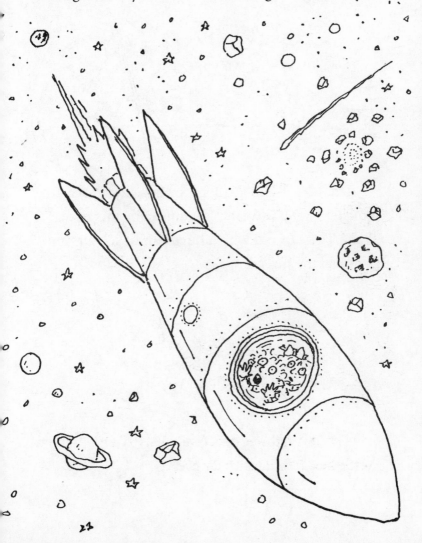

27

"Don't worry, Hansel," replied Gretel. "Look at the new sweater Father made for me… It is getting smaller and smaller. That's because I tied one end to a nail on Luna's shed, and now my sweater is unwinding behind us."

It was true! The further they flew into space, the smaller Gretel's sweater became. Only this time, Luna Tick ran out with a huge pair of scissors and snipped the thread!

"Ah haaar haar harr!"

The rocket blasted further and further into outer space – further than any child had ever been before.

"I am frightened, Hansy," said Gretel.

"I am frightened too, Grety," said Hansel.

To their horror, they saw that the rocket had run out of fuel. Now they were drifting, lost and alone in outer space.

Then the children saw something very strange flashing through the starry sky. It looked like a broomstick! But the broomstick was longer than their space rocket. In the front of the broomstick was a glass cockpit, and inside the cockpit was an enormous alien creature with a long nose tied in a knot on her hideous green face. They heard a crackly voice on the radio –

Cackle cackle, shake and twitch
Come and fly with the old SPACE WITCH!

Hansel and Gretel knew they should never take a lift from strangers. But what else could they do? They put on their space helmets, opened the rocket door, and floated across to the flying broom.

Cackle cackle, step inside
Little broom mates, take A RIDE!

Before they knew what was happening, the evil
Space Witch locked the door, pushed a lever and
the broomstick shot away into the dark sky.

"Help, help!" squealed Hansel and Gretel. But it was too late. They were locked inside the flying broom.

Cackle cackle, please don't whine Little children, now YOU'RE MINE!

After a long and terrifying journey, they arrived at a strange planet, where the sky was filled with multi-coloured clouds, which glowed in the dark. The children looked down and saw that the whole planet was covered with small smoking volcanoes.

The Space Witch landed the flying broom beside a gleaming glass dome. She dragged the poor children inside.

Cackle cackle, welcome home
You'll spend your life in the
SPACE WITCH DOME!

In the dome was a kitchen where the table was set for lunch. In the middle of the room was a red-hot volcano with a cooking pot on top.

"Gulp!" said Hansel." I wonder what she eats?"

Cackle cackle, munch munch munch
I'll go outside and catch some lunch

She gave Hansel and Gretel a broom each and made them sweep the floor. Then the Space Witch picked up a long net and went outside the dome.

To the children's amazement, she reached up and
caught one of the glowing clouds. She brought
it inside and was just about to shove it into the
cooking pot, when the cloud said –

"BAAA!"

"Oh!" gasped Gretel. "Those clouds are not clouds. Look, Hansel, they are Glow-in-the-Dark Space Sheep!"

"Poor little thing," said Hansel. "Isn't there anything else to eat on this planet?"

An evil grin spread across the face of the Space Witch. She dropped the sheep and looked hungrily at Hansel.

Cackle, cackle! What I enjoy is a lovely slice of FRESH COOKED BOY!

The horrible Space Witch was just about to grab Hansel, when, quick as a flash, Gretel jumped forward and swept her into the volcano.

Cackle, crackle, flames and flickers
There's red hot lava in my knickers!

"All right, don't fly off the handle!" said Gretel.

"That's what I call broom service!" said Hansel.

The children picked up the little space sheep, put on their helmets, and grabbed the keys to the flying broom.

"Time to go home," shouted Gretel.

She typed their postcode into the sat nav and the broom went hurtling through space.

Far ahead of them, they saw a little blue and green planet.

"It's earth!" said Hansel.

"We're going home!" said Gretel. "Baaa!" said the Glow-in-the-Dark Space Sheep.

Early the next morning, Hansel and Gretel landed the Flying Broom in the garden of their father's house. Larry Lambsbottom was overjoyed to see his beautiful children.

Of course, Luna was furious, but she calmed down when the children gave her the keys to the Flying Broom.

"Perhaps you should fly away for a spell," said Hansel and Gretel.

And that was the terrifying story of the evil Space Witch. Every word was true.

Oh, I forgot to mention – with the help of their pet Space Sheep, Larry began knitting multi-coloured Glow-in-the Dark sweaters. They were so popular, that the family became rich beyond their wildest dreams.

SERIOUSLY SILLY

SCARY
FAIRY TALES

LAURENCE ANHOLT & ARTHUR ROBINS

Cinderella at the Vampire Ball   PB 978 1 40832 954 2

Jack and the Giant Spiderweb   PB 978 1 40832 957 3

Hansel and Gretel and the Space Witch   PB 978 1 40832 960 3

Snow Fright and the Seven Skeletons   PB 978 1 40832 963 4

Ghostyshocks and the Three Mummies   PB 978 1 40832 966 5

Tom Thumb the Tiny Spook   PB 978 1 40832 969 6

COLLECT THEM ALL!

Also available
as an ebook